To Jonah, Lennox, and Augustine.
Off you go, little ones.

Balzer + Bray is an imprint of HarperCollins Publishers.

The Digger and the Duckling
Copyright © 2022 by Joseph Kuefler
All rights reserved. Manufactured in Italy.
No part of this book may be used or reproduced in any manner whatsoever without
written permission except in the case of brief quotations embodied in critical articles
and reviews. For information address HarperCollins Children's Books, a division of
HarperCollins Publishers, 195 Broadway, New York, NY 10007.
www.harpercollinschildrens.com

Library of Congress Control Number: 2021939647
ISBN 978-0-06-306254-2

Typography by Joseph Kuefler and Dana Fritts
21 22 23 24 25   RTLO   10 9 8 7 6 5 4 3 2 1
❖
First Edition

THE
DIGGER
AND THE
DUCKLING

JOSEPH KUEFLER

BALZER + BRAY
An Imprint of HarperCollinsPublishers

Digger and his crew loved to work.

Each day, they rolled. And hoisted.
And dug. And built.

One day, a lost duckling appeared.
She waddled and quacked and
wandered through the jobsite.

"That duckling is blocking my blade," said Dozer.

"That duckling is pooing on my polish," said Mixie.

"That duckling is a nuisance," said Crane.

The other big trucks agreed.
But Digger did not.
"She is not a nuisance," said Digger.
"She is looking for her mother."

"We are not mothers," said Crane. "We are big trucks."

"We do not babysit," said Dozer. "We build."

"That duckling must go," said Roller.

When the workday was done, Digger
drove the duckling to the edge of the city.

"Off you go, little one," said Digger.
But the duckling waddled right back
into Digger's scoop.

Quack quack, said the duckling.
Digger smiled. "You can stay for tonight.
Tomorrow your mother will come."

The next day, the big trucks were back at work.
Smashing. Hauling. Hoisting. Building.

Wherever Digger drove, the duckling followed.

"She waddled through our road," said Roller.
"She ruined our work," said Hauler.
"She is more than a nuisance," said Crane.
"That duckling is trouble."

The other big trucks agreed . . .

But Digger and Squirt did not.

"She is not trouble," said Squirt. "She is just looking for some water."
"We can build her a pond," said Digger.
Quack quack, said the duckling.

Digger scooped.

Squirt sprayed.

And the two big trucks built
the duckling a pond.

"Off you go, little one," said Digger.

She paddled and bobbed until her legs grew tired.
"Tomorrow your mother will return," said Squirt.

Many tomorrows came and went.

Each day, the duckling worked alongside the big trucks.

She helped Scoops scoop.

She helped Mixie mix.

She helped Hauler haul.

"What a worker," said Roller.
The other big trucks agreed.

"She's more than a worker," said Crane.
"She's a builder."

Together, the crew cared for the duckling.

They filled her belly.

They cleaned her feathers.

They played and played.

Spring became summer.

The duckling became a duck.

And the crew became a family.

One day in late summer, a great wind whipped up.
It bent the trees and shook the buildings.

"She is not safe," said Digger. "We should take a break."
The other big trucks agreed.

But the great wind whipped again.
A whip so strong it rattled Digger's rivets
and blew the duck out of Digger's scoop.

The big trucks went to work.
"Catch her!" said Hauler.
"Hook her!" said Crane.
"Save her!" said Digger.

Before the big trucks
could catch her . . .

She spread her wings and flew.
High into the air and

back into Digger's scoop.
The big trucks cheered.

But Digger did not.
He realized their duck was grown now.
"Your future is out there," said Digger.

Quack quack, said the duck.
"Quack quack," said the big trucks.

The wind picked up again.
The duck turned to the south and flew.

The big trucks smiled proudly as they
watched her go.

The seasons changed. The big trucks built.

All the while they thought of the duck, hoping
she would return. And then one day . . .

She did.